Davy

Manni

Lina

P9-DMW-331

Brigitte Weninger was born in Kufstein, Austria, and spent twenty years working as a kindergarten teacher before trying her hand at writing. She has since published more than fifty books, which have been translated into thirty languages worldwide. She continues to be heavily involved in promoting literacy and storytelling.

Eve Tharlet was born in France but spent much of her childhood in Germany. After graduating from the Superior School of Decorative Arts in Strasbourg, France, she began working as a freelance illustrator in 1981 and quickly received international acclaim. Her big breakthrough came with the series about Davy, the cute and cheeky bunny, which propelled her name around the world.

Copyright © 2000 by NordSüd Verlag AG, CH-8005, Zürich, Switzerland.
First published in Switzerland under the title *Herzlichen Glückwunsch, Pauli.*
English translation copyright © 2000 by NorthSouth Books, Inc., New York 10016.
Translated by Rosemary Lanning

All rights reserved.
No part of this book may be reproduced or utilized in any form or by any means, electronic or mechanical, including photo-copying, recording, or any information storage and retrieval system, without permission in writing from the publisher.

First published in the United States, Great Britain, Canada, Australia, and New Zealand in 2000 by NorthSouth Books, Inc., an imprint of NordSüd Verlag AG, CH-8005 Zürich, Switzerland. This edition published in 2015 by NorthSouth Books.

Distributed in the United States by NorthSouth Books, Inc., New York 10016.
Library of Congress Cataloging-in-Publication Data is available.
ISBN: 978-0-7358-4224-3 (trade edition)
1 3 5 7 9 • 10 8 6 4 2
Printed in Germany by Grafisches Centrum Cuno GmbH & Co. KG, Calbe, April 2015

www.northsouth.com

FSC
www.fsc.org
MIX
Paper from responsible sources
FSC® C043106

Happy
Birthday,
Davy!

Brigitte Weninger • illustrated by Eve Tharlet

Translated by Rosemary Lanning

"How much longer
is it till my birthday?"
asked Davy.

"You've asked me that a hundred times," said Mother Rabbit, hiding a smile.

"I know," said Davy. "But how much longer?"

"Ten more days," said Mother.

"That long?" cried Davy.

But soon it was seven more days, then five, then three. . . .
Davy was so excited he couldn't sit still.

Father Rabbit was telling them a story about a little rabbit
who had three wishes: ". . . so all his wishes came true, and
he hopped happily back to his burrow."

"I love that story," said Lina. "Tell it again, please!"

"No. I'm sorry. I have work to do," said Father Rabbit.

"Oh!" said Davy with a disappointed sigh. "If I had a
wish I would ask for someone who always had time to tell
stories."

The next morning it rained so hard that the rabbit children had to stay indoors. By the afternoon they had run out of things to do.

"Let's play tag," suggested Manni.

"We've played that already," said Max.

"Want to play ball!" squeaked little Mia.

But they soon got bored with that too.

Davy stared gloomily out at the rain.

"If *I* had a wish," he muttered, "I would ask for someone to teach us more games."

The following morning Davy couldn't find anyone who had time to play. They were all too busy getting ready for his birthday. Davy was pleased about that, but he was bored on his own.

"You know, Nicky," he said to his toy rabbit, "if *I* had a wish, I would ask for someone who had lots of time to spend with me."

At last it was Davy's birthday!
He woke to hear the whole
family singing,

"Happy Birthday, dear Davy!"

Max had made him a beautiful
garland. "When you wear this,
everyone will know it's your birthday,"
he said.

"Thank you!" said Davy. "It's great!"

He had to wait until his party that
afternoon for the rest of his presents.
Waiting was very hard!

Finally it was time for the party, but where were the presents?

"Davy dear, Mother and I listened to all your wishes," said Father, smiling, "but the present we chose was much too big to wrap. So we hid it somewhere in the burrow. See if you can find it!"

Davy's heart began to pound. Could his present really be that big? What could it be? He looked around the room, but he couldn't see anything. There was no present in his bedroom. Was it under Mother Rabbit's bed? No! But there was something behind the pantry door. . . .

"Grandpa! Granny!" Davy gave
them both a hug.

"Many happy returns of the day, Davy
dear," said his grandparents, laughing.
"We are your birthday present this
year, and we have brought a whole
sackful of time with us. Time for stories,
time for games, and time for anything
else you want to do."

There were still more presents
for Davy: a shiny pebble from Eddie,
a toy tea set from Lina and Manni,
which they had made themselves,
and a kiss and hug from Mia. Grandpa
and Granny gave him a big book
of stories.

"Now we can read you a new story
every day," said Mother.

"But what will we do when
we have read them all?"
asked Davy anxiously.

"We'll go back to the
beginning again!"
said Father. "A good story
is worth repeating."

"Now we'll teach you the games we played when we were young," said Grandpa.

He and Granny showed the children how to play Simon Says and statues and musical chairs. And they played until Mother called them for supper. Then they played some more. Davy didn't win many games, but he didn't mind at all. He was happy.

After supper the birthday boy
was allowed to choose a story.
He held the new storybook
while Grandpa read aloud, and
everyone listened, enthralled.

Then Granny told the children all
about the pranks she and Grandpa
used to play when they were young.
Davy liked those stories best of all.
   By now the children were very
tired. It had been a long, exciting day.

Only Davy was still awake. "That was my best birthday ever," he whispered to his grandparents.

"And when it's your birthday, you can wish for a little rabbit to play with you and love you. Then I will come and be your birthday present."

"What a good idea," said Granny as Davy snuggled in Grandpa's arms and fell fast asleep.